To Katie

First published 2003 by Walker Books Ltd
87 Vauxhall Walk, London SE11 5HJ

2 4 6 8 10 9 7 5 3 1

© 2003 Charlotte Voake

The right of Charlotte Voake to be identified as
author/illustrator of this work has been asserted by her in
accordance with the Copyright, Designs and Patents Act 1988

This book has been typeset in Calligraphic

Printed in Hong Kong

British Library Cataloguing in Publication Data:
a catalogue record for this book is available
from the British Library

ISBN 0-7445-9648-3

GINGER
finds a home

Charlotte Voake

WALKER BOOKS
AND SUBSIDIARIES
LONDON • BOSTON • SYDNEY

Once there was
a little ginger cat
who lived in
a patch of weeds
at the bottom
of a garden.

His ears were black
with dirt. He was very thin.
His fur stuck out.

His tail was like
a piece of
STRING!

He drank water
out of puddles.
He looked in dustbins
for things to eat.

Every day he searched
for food,
and every night,
he went back
to his patch of weeds
to sleep.

Then one day,
everything
changed.

The little cat had found
nothing to eat except
a bit of bread,
and he was cold
and hungry as he
came back to bed.

He stopped.
There on the
ground was ...

a delicious
plate of
cat food!

He couldn't believe his eyes!

He gobbled it up
and went to sleep.
He had never
slept so well!

The next night,
he found another
plate of food
waiting
for him ...

and SOMETHING
ELSE.

A little
girl!

"Hello,"
she said.

She tried to stroke his fur,
but he was
frightened,
and ran
to hide
in the
weeds.

"See you tomorrow,"
said the little girl.

She came to visit
him every day.
She brought him
lovely things
to eat.

She
called him
Ginger.

Soon Ginger looked forward to seeing the little girl. He came when she called, and when she stroked him, he purred.

The little girl loved Ginger.

"Ginger," she said.
"You can't stay here.
Why don't you
come home
with me?"

So Ginger followed
the little girl
home.

He had never
been in a house before.

He looked
in all the
corners and
under all
the furniture.
But poor
Ginger
was
so nervous ...

that when the little girl
tried to shut
the door,

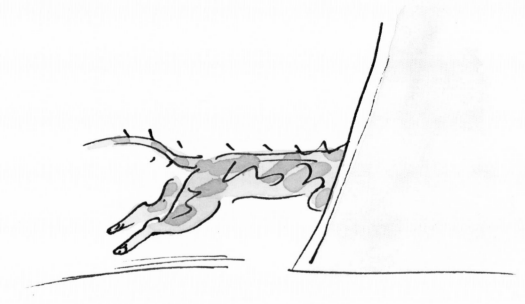

he ran out into
the garden as fast as he could.

The little girl
looked outside.
She couldn't
see him
anywhere.
"Ginger!"
she called.

But Ginger didn't come.

"I've frightened him away," she said. "He doesn't want to live with me."

The little girl
	was very sad.
	She was so upset,
		she didn't notice ...

when Ginger came
creeping back in.

"Miaow!"

said Ginger.

"GINGER!"

said the little girl.

Now Ginger lives with the little girl in her house.

He is a very happy cat.

And the only time
he ever goes back
to the patch of weeds
at the bottom
of the garden …

is to

sunbathe!